the Littlest Dragon

Goes for Goal

Roaring Good Reads will fire the imagination of all
young readers – from short stories for children just
starting to read on their own, to first chapter books and short
novels for confident readers.

www.roaringgoodreads.co.uk

Other exciting titles available in the Roaring Good Read series:

*Short, lively stories, with illustrations on every page,
for children just starting to read by themselves*

Morris the Mouse Hunter *Vivian French*
Morris and the Cat Flap *Vivian French*
Morris in the Apple Tree *Vivian French*
The Littlest Dragon *Margaret Ryan*

*For confident readers, with short chapters and
illustrations throughout*

Daisy May *Jean Ure*
Dazzling Danny *Jean Ure*
Down with the Dirty Danes *Gillian Cross*
The Gargling Gorilla *Margaret Mahy*
Happy Birthday, Spider McDrew *Alan Durant*
King Henry VIII's Shoes *Karen Wallace*
Lilac Peabody and Sam Sparks *Annie Dalton*
Mr Skip *Michael Morpurgo*
Muckabout School *Ian Whybrow*
Spider McDrew *Alan Durant*
Witch-in-Training: Flying Lessons *Maeve Friel*
Witch-in-Training: Spelling Trouble *Maeve Friel*
Witch-in-Training: Charming or What? *Maeve Friel*
Witch-in-Training: Brewing Up *Maeve Friel*
The Witch's Tears *Jenny Nimmo*

the Littlest Dragon

Goes for Goal

Margaret Ryan

Illustrations by Jamie Smith

ROARING GOOD READS

Collins

An imprint of HarperCollins*Publishers*

First published in Great Britain by Collins in 1999
This edition published in Great Britain by HarperCollins*Children'sBooks* 2004
HarperCollins*Children'sBooks* is an imprint of HarperCollins*Publishers* Ltd
77-85 Fulham Palace Road, Hammersmith, London W6 8JB

The HarperCollins*Children'sBooks* website address is
www.harpercollinschildrensbooks.co.uk

1 3 5 7 9 8 6 4 2

Text copyright © Margaret Ryan 1999
Illustrations © Jamie Smith 1999

ISBN 0 00 719294 0

The author and illustrator assert the moral right
to be identified as the author and illustrator of the work.

Printed and bound in England by
Clays Ltd, St Ives plc

Contents

Happy Birthday, Littlest Dragon

It was a very special day. In the dragons' cave, ten dragons lay in the big dragons' bed. Nine of the dragons were fast asleep, but the littlest one, Number Ten, was wide awake.

"I wonder what the postman will bring me today," he said, and jumped out of bed to see.

"Happy Birthday, Number Ten," said the postman. "Here are all your cards and parcels. Have a nice day!"

"I will," said the littlest dragon. "My cousin, Emerald, is coming over soon. We're going to play with all my presents."

"I'm here already," yelled Emerald,
bumping up the path on her bike.
"Happy birthday, Number Ten.
Look what I got you!"

"Chocolate toffees. Yummy!" said Number Ten. "Thanks, Em. We'll eat these now, then we can watch my new football video and play my new computer game."

The littlest dragon opened up the box of chocolate toffees and was just about to reach in when...

"I thought I could smell chocolate toffees," said big dragon brother, Number One.

"I can always sniff out chocolate toffees," said big dragon brother, Number Two.

"So can we," said all the other dragon brothers, and grabbed the box.

11

"But they're MY toffees," said Number Ten. "I got them for MY birthday."

"Remember to share," laughed all the dragon brothers and started to eat the sweets.

By the time the littlest dragon got the
box back, only the wrappers were left.

"This won't do," muttered the littlest
dragon. "This won't do at all."

Then he had his first idea.

"Come on, Emerald," he whispered. "We'll go and watch my new football video while they're busy munching."

The littlest dragon put on the video and he and Emerald were just about to watch it when...

"A new football video. Brilliant," said big dragon brother, Number Four.

"We love football videos," said twins, Five and Six.

"Shove along, Number Ten, so we can see," said big brothers One, Two and Three.

"But now Emerald and I can't see," said the littlest dragon, as they were pushed THUMP on to the floor, and elbowed OUCH to the back of the room. "And it's MY video. I got it for MY birthday."

"Remember to share," laughed all the other dragon brothers, and jumped up to cheer when a goal was scored.

"This won't do," muttered the littlest dragon. "This won't do at all."

Then he had his second idea.

"Come on, Emerald," he whispered.
"We'll go and play with my new computer
game while they're busy watching."

The littlest dragon switched on the computer, loaded his game, and then he and Emerald began to play.

They were both just getting a really high score when...

"A new computer game. Cool," said big dragon brother, Number Nine.

"I love computer games," said big dragon brother, Number Three.

"Shove over, Number Ten, it's our turn next," said twin dragon brothers, Five and Six.

"But now Emerald and I can't play," said Number Ten, as they were pushed THUMP on to the floor, and elbowed OUCH to the back of the room. "And it's MY game. I got it for MY birthday."

"Remember to share," laughed all the other dragon brothers, and fought over who should be first to play.

The littlest dragon took Emerald's hand
and stomped into the big cave kitchen.

"It's not fair," he muttered.

"What's not fair, Number Ten?" asked his mum, who was busy making his special birthday cake.

"It's not fair that we can't get to play with MY birthday presents on MY birthday. Just because we're the littlest."

Then his mum had an idea.

"Why don't you and Emerald mix up this birthday cake while I go and have a word with these big brothers," she said.

"OK," said the littlest dragon.

Then he had his third and naughtiest idea.

"Come on Emerald," he whispered. "We'll mix salt into the cake instead of sugar while the others are busy playing."

"That's your best idea yet, Number Ten," giggled Emerald.

Soon the littlest dragon's mum came
back and popped the cake in the oven.

When it was ready, the littlest dragon
was just blowing out the candles when...

"I thought I could smell birthday cake," said big dragon brother, Number One.

"I can always sniff out birthday cake," said big brother, Number Two.

"So can we," said all the other dragon
brothers, and cut themselves such huge
slices that there was none left for the
littlest dragon or Emerald.

"What about us?" asked the littlest
dragon. "It's MY cake. It was made for
MY birthday."

"Remember to share," laughed all the
dragon brothers, and took enormous
bites of the cake.

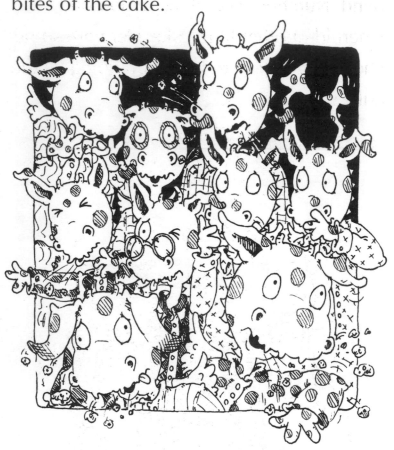

"EEK ARRRGH OOH YUK!!!!" they all
yelled, and ran outside holding their
throats and their tums.

"Oh dear," said their mum. "I'm always telling them not to be so greedy. Never mind, Number Ten, I'll make you and Emerald another little cake. Here are some chocolate toffees to keep you going till the cake's ready."

"Thanks, Mum," said the littlest dragon, and he shared the toffees with Emerald.

"We'll eat these now," he grinned. "Then we can watch my new football video and play my new computer game!"

The Littlest Dragon Goes for Goal

It was Saturday afternoon. In the dragons' cave, the ten dragon brothers were getting ready to go to the next field to watch their favourite football star, Dragon McFeet, play his weekly game.

"I'm wearing the special winning jersey Dragon McFeet gave me," said the littlest dragon. "Pity I've only got these old boots of Number Nine's."

He was just lacing up the old boots
when his nine dragon brothers thundered
past him on their way to the game.

"Wait for me," yelled the littlest
dragon, tripping over his laces.

The dragon brothers found a good spot
behind the goal, and clapped and cheered
as Dragon McFeet scored the winning goal.

Then Dragon McFeet made a special
announcement.

"At next week's game," he said, "my
boots will be raffled to raise money for
the Baby Dragons' Hospital. I hope you
will all buy a ticket."

"We will," said dragon brothers, One and Two.

"Yes, yes," said Three and Four.

"We'll run home right now and empty our dragon banks," said twin dragon brothers, Five and Six.

"Wait for me," cried the littlest dragon, as nine dragon brothers thundered past him back to the dragons' cave.

The littlest dragon tripped along behind. But when he got home, his brothers were looking miserable.

"My dragon bank's empty," said
Number Eight.

"I've only got a button left," said
Number Seven.

"I found a hairy toffee in mine," said
Number Two.

The littlest dragon smiled and got out his
dragon bank.

"There's still some birthday money in
mine," he said.

But there wasn't. Instead there were some letters which said...

Dear Number Ten,

I borrowed some money for football stickers. Will pay you back soon.

Love,

Number Three.

Dear Number Ten,

I borrowed some money for lollipops. will pay you back soon.

Love,

Number Nine.

Dear Number Ten,

we borrowed some money for dribbly chocolate ice cream. we love dribbly chocolate ice cream. will pay you back soon.

Love,

the twins (Five and Six).

"Oh no," said the littlest dragon. "How will I be able to buy a raffle ticket for Dragon McFeet's boots?"

Then he had his first idea.

"I'll go and ask Mum if she needs any jobs done in the house," he said. "That way I can earn some money to buy a raffle ticket."

"Good idea, Number Ten," said his
nine dragon brothers, and thundered
past him into the kitchen.

"Wait for me," cried the littlest dragon.
"It was MY idea."

But by the time he got to ask his mum what he could do to earn some money, there was only cleaning the smelly wellies left.

"I hate cleaning the smelly wellies," said Number Ten. "Why do dragons have such smelly feet?"

The dragon brothers' smelly wellies were kept outside the back door, so the littlest dragon picked up the garden hose and scooted them with water.

Then he went back into the kitchen.

"Any more jobs, Mum?"

"No, that's all," said his mum, and gave him some money.

But he still didn't have enough to buy a raffle ticket.

Then he had his second idea.

"I'll go and ask Dad if he needs any jobs done in the garden," he said.

"Good idea, Number Ten," said his nine dragon brothers, and thundered past him into the garden.

"Wait for me," cried the littlest dragon. "It was MY idea."

But by the time he got to ask his dad
what he could do to earn some money,
there was only the muck spreading left.

"I hate muck spreading," said Number
Ten. "Why do flowers need such smelly
stuff to make them grow?"

He got out his red plastic spade from the cupboard in the hall, and huffed and puffed till he had covered the flower beds in muck. Then the littlest dragon's dad gave all the dragons the money they had earned.

"Wait for me," yelled the littlest dragon as his nine dragon brothers thundered past him on their way to the shop to buy their raffle tickets.

The littlest dragon tripped along behind, and got the very last one.

He couldn't wait for Saturday to arrive. As usual, the dragon brothers went to the game in the next field. They saw Dragon McFeet score the winning goal.

Then, when the game was over,
Dragon McFeet picked out the winning
raffle ticket.

"It's number... ten," he said.

"That's mine, that's mine!" cried the
littlest dragon, and he ran out on to the
field to get his prize.

He wore Dragon McFeet's winning
boots, which were far too big for him,
all the way home.

Next day, the dragon brothers went out to play their usual game of football. The littlest dragon wore the winning boots, but, every time he kicked the ball, the boots flew into the air too.

"Those boots are far too big for you,
Number Ten," said Number One. "Better
let me wear them."

"No, me," said Number Two. "I'm sure
they're my size."

"What about me, and me, and me?" said
the other dragons.

But then the littlest dragon had his third and smelliest idea. He hung the boots round his neck, put clothes pegs on his nose, and went and stood in the muck heap.

"If it can make the flowers grow," he squeaked, "perhaps it can do the same for my feet!"

Two more stories about the
Littlest Dragon with the Big Ideas

the Littlest Dragon

Margaret Ryan

Illustrated by Jamie Smith

*It's hard being the youngest
in the family – especially when
you've got nine older brothers!*

Find out how the Littlest Dragon
manages to get a peaceful night's
sleep in the dragons' bed. And
discover how he manages to get a very
special winning football shirt... for free!

ISBN 0 00 714163 7

ROARING GOOD READS

Collins

An imprint of HarperCollinsPublishers

www.roaringgoodreads.co.uk

MORRIS
AND THE CAT FLAP

Vivian French

Illustrations by Olivia Villet

Meet Morris – the greediest cat in the world!

Morris is outside. His food is inside!
Morris is scared.
He doesn't like the cat flap.
He thinks it might chop his tail off.
Only something very special
will make him change his mind.

ISBN 0 00 714161 0

ROARING GOOD READS

Collins

An imprint of HarperCollins*Publishers*

www.roaringgoodreads.co.uk

Victoria Lloyd

Illustrated by Scott Walker

Liar! Liar! Pants on Fire!

Tony has the coolest pair of pants in school. But they're not ordinary pants; when Tony tells a little lie, they start to get warm. And when he tells a whopping great lie, they get really HOT. How can Tony keep his cool – and his pants...

ISBN 0 00 715525 5

An imprint of HarperCollins*Publishers*

www.roaringgoodreads.co.uk